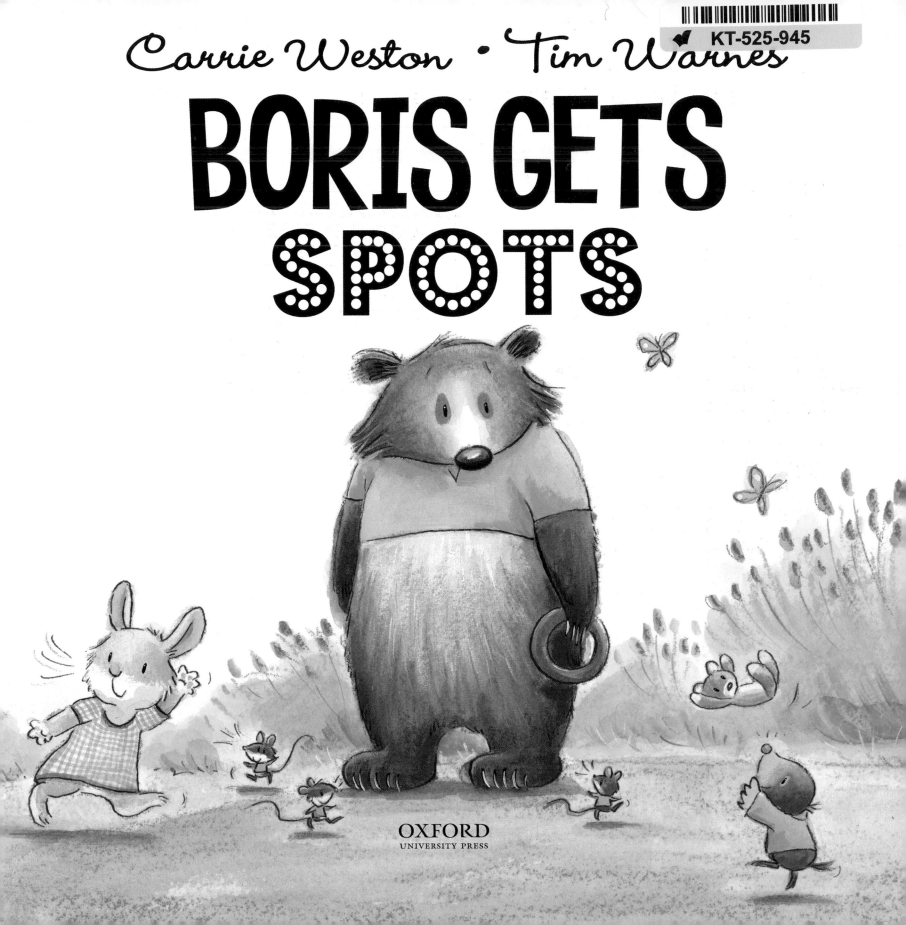

Carrie Weston • Tim Warnes

BORIS GETS
SPOTS

OXFORD
UNIVERSITY PRESS

The day that Miss Cluck said
there was going to be a
special visitor everyone was
very excited.

When she said it was Mr Gander
from Gosling Farm there were
squeals of delight.

Fergus the fox cub made
his best farm noises.

Leticia the rabbit
burst into song.

Maxwell the mole showed everyone how to barn dance.
The little mice skipped like lambs.

But Boris asked if he could sit quietly in the book corner.

'Of course, dear,'
said Miss Cluck kindly.

'What's wrong
with Boris?'

Just then, there was a loud 'moo!' outside.

It was Buttercup the cow from Gosling Farm!

'Good morning, children!' smiled Mr Gander, raising his straw hat. 'Who would like to see what I've brought? Fresh from the farm!'

'Me!'

'And me!'

'Me too!'

Miss Cluck and her class gathered around the cart.

First, Mr Gander brought down a basket. 'These eggs were laid this morning,' he said.

'Oooh!'

Maxwell gently lifted an egg out of the straw. It was still warm.

Next, Mr Gander passed round a fluffy blanket.
'Made of wool from my sheep,' he explained.
Leticia held it against her cheek.

Then he let everyone taste the honey from his bees.

Mr Gander brought out fresh milk and butter
and told them all about the dairy.

He poured out flour and oats
and told them about the grain store.

It gave Miss Cluck an idea.
'Let's make some honey
cookies,' she said, 'to say
"thank you" to Mr Gander.'

'Yippee!'

'Hooray!'

Suddenly, Maxwell stopped. 'Where's Boris?' he asked.
'Oh!' said Miss Cluck. 'He must still be in the book corner!'

'I'll tell him about the cookies!' said Fergus.
'He loves honey!'

A moment later there was
a cry from the classroom
'Miss Cluck!' yelled Fergus.
'Boris is covered in spots!'

Everyone rushed inside.
Everyone stopped.
Everyone stared.

For poor Boris had red spots all over his nose and feet.

Book Corner

'They itch, Miss!'

Non-fiction titles

'Oh, Boris!' exclaimed Miss Cluck,
'I think you have chicken pox!'

The little animals gasped.

'Boris has chitten pops!'

How many apples can you see hanging from the tree?

How many green apples?

How many red apples?

How many yellow apples?

1 2 3 4 5 6 7 8

'Oh no!'

'Hush,' said Miss Cluck. 'There's no need for alarm. Almost everyone gets chicken pox just once,' she explained getting out the first-aid box.

Inside she found some cooling lotion for Boris's itchy spots.

Mr Gander offered Boris a spoonful of honey
and the woolly blanket to wrap up in.
Just then, Leticia yawned. She was feeling sleepy.

'Look!' said Fergus. 'Leticia has spots, too!'
'Oh dear!' said Miss Cluck. 'I think we'd better
make room next to Boris.'

'Can we make a get-well-soon card?' asked Maxwell.

'What a lovely idea,' said Miss Cluck.

The animals got out paper and crayons. Everyone was very busy. Until . . . there was a loud squeal.

Pass scissors handle first to your friends.

Fergus pointed at Maxwell.

Maxwell pointed at the mice.

The mice pointed at Fergus.

'More spots!' they yelled.

'Oh goodness gracious,' said Miss Cluck.

'I think everyone needs to be tucked up in bed.'

Mr Gander agreed and Buttercup was ready to take the animals home. It was quite a squeeze in the cart, but nobody minded a bit. After all, they were all feeling poorly.

Miss Cluck waved goodbye as Buttercup set off. 'Get well soon!' she called.

The next day Miss Cluck tidied the books, put up some paintings, and fed the goldfish. It seemed far too quiet and lonely in the empty classroom.

Sigh!

She looked at all the things Mr Gander had brought.
It was such a shame that the animals had
missed out on making their honey cookies.

But then Miss Cluck
had a **brilliant** idea.

She put 100g of soft butter into a large bowl. Then she poured in two big spoonfuls of runny honey and beat hard.

Next she added 75g of flour, 100g of oats, 75g of brown sugar, and half a teaspoon of baking powder. She mixed everything together.

Honey Cookies

You will need:
100 g butter
2 tbsp runny honey
75 g flour
100 g oats
75 g brown sugar
1/2 tsp baking powder

step 1
Add 2 big spoonfuls of runny honey to the butter and mix well

Finally, she sprinkled some flour on the table and rolled out little balls of dough.

They were ready to pop into the oven at 180°C.
'I think about 20 minutes should do,'
said Miss Cluck to herself.

When the cookies were done, Miss Cluck
left them to cool before putting them
into special boxes at the end of the day.

As she turned out the lights, she hoped the
animals would be back to enjoy them in the morning.

And they were!
Through the gate came Mr Gander,
followed by Boris, and finally Buttercup,
who had all the little animals on her back.
And nobody had any spots at all!

'Moo!

Moo!'

Miss Cluck was delighted
to see her class
looking better.

'I have a special treat for
you all!' she beamed.

The animals sat in a circle and Miss Cluck
passed round the cookies.

Afterwards, Mr Gander played his harmonica and there was singing and dancing all around the classroom.

It was very noisy indeed but Miss Cluck didn't mind one little bit . . .

after all, she was so glad
to have **everyone** back.